In Loving Memory

Of

Carolyn Baker

Senior English Teacher

The Adventures of SHERLOCK HOLMES

Sir Arthur Conan Doyle

Abridged and adapted by Jeff Whitmore
Illustrated by Laurie Harden

A PACEMAKER CLASSIC

GLOBE FEARON
Pearson Learning Group

Project Editor: Ann Clarkson
Senior Editor: Lynn Kloss
Editorial Assistant: Daniel Heavener
Designer: Lisa Nuland
Production Editor: Alan Dalgleish
Composition: Phyllis Rosinsky
Illustrator: Laurie Harden

Sherlock Holmes was created by the late Sir Arthur
Conan Doyle, and appears in stories and novels by him.
Grateful acknowledgement to the Estate of Dame Jean
Conan Doyle for permission to adapt the stories
contained in this edition.

ISBN 0-835-93592-2

Printed in the United States of America
    7 8 9 10   06 05

Contents

Preface

Sherlock Holmes is familiar to readers around the world. The master detective faced some of the worst criminals of his time. And he outsmarted them all.

Arthur Conan Doyle created the character Sherlock Holmes in 1887. Holmes is now probably the most famous detective in literature. He was both brave and clever. He often used his intelligence to solve mysteries that baffled the police.

Dr. John Watson is as famous as Holmes. He is the detective's loyal friend and able assistant. We learn of Holmes's adventures through Watson's words.

Holmes and Watson had shared rooms at 221B Baker Street in London. Then Watson moved out after he married. Later, after his wife died, he moved back to Baker Street.

The stories are filled with action, mystery, humor, and excitement. Readers have always enjoyed trying to solve the mysteries along with Holmes. Perhaps you will, too.

The Adventure of the Speckled Band

My name is Dr. John Watson. For many years, Sherlock Holmes and I shared rooms at 221B Baker Street in London. Our landlady was a kindly woman named Mrs. Hudson. You may have heard of Sherlock Holmes. He is a famous detective.

I awoke early one morning in April 1883. Standing by my bed was Sherlock Holmes.

"Watson," he said, "I am very sorry to wake you, but we have a visitor. When a young lady is traveling in the city this early, it must be for an interesting cause."

"I am sure," I agreed, looking at the clock. It was just past seven. I dressed quickly and went downstairs with Holmes to meet our unexpected guest.

She was dressed all in black and seemed to be shaking from the cold. Holmes said, "Good morning, Madam. I am Sherlock Holmes, and this is my trusted friend Dr. Watson. I will have Mrs. Hudson bring us some coffee. That and the fire should warm you."

"It is not the cold that makes me shake," the young woman explained. "It is fear."

She lifted her head, and we could see the fear in her face. Her skin was pale, and her eyes were like those of a hunted animal. I guessed she was about 30, but there was much gray in her hair. She looked as though she hadn't slept in a long time.

Holmes looked her over quickly, but carefully. "You must not fear," he said. "We will soon set things right." He tipped his head to one side. "Well," he added, "I see you got up early this morning and came to London by train."

"How did you know that?" The young woman raised her eyebrows.

"I can see you have half of a return train ticket tucked into your glove. I also see that you must have traveled to the station in a small open carriage on a very rough road."

The lady looked at Holmes in surprise.

He smiled and said, "There is no mystery to it, Madam. I see there is newly dried mud on your left arm. Only such a carriage would throw up mud that way. And, of course, only if you sat on the left side of the driver."

"You are right," she said. "I can see that what I have heard about you is true. You have great powers of detection. Now, sir, I beg you to help me. You once helped my friend Mrs. Farintosh, and she gave me your name. Maybe you can shed a little light on the darkness that surrounds me. I can't pay you now. But in a month I will marry and inherit some money."

Holmes nodded, "Farintosh. I remember her case. If you can pay my expenses after your marriage, it will be helpful. But for me, solving interesting cases is my real reward. Now tell me everything you can about your case. Go into detail. I promise I will give you my full attention."

"My name is Helen Stoner," she said. "I live with my stepfather, Dr. Grimesby Roylott. He is the last living member of the Roylott family. The Roylotts were once a wealthy family, but their money was wasted. Now, only the Roylott estate, Stoke Moran, remains.

"Years ago, my stepfather was a doctor in India. He married my mother. My father, Major General Stoner, had died in battle. While in India, Dr. Roylott killed a servant he believed to be a burglar. He was put in prison. When he was released, we all moved back to England. Dr. Roylott planned to open a practice in London. Soon after that, my mother was killed in a train accident. Dr. Roylott gave up his plan. Instead, he took my twin sister, Julia, and me to Stoke Moran to live with him."

"I have heard of the estate," said Holmes.

"My mother's will left an income of 1,000 pounds a year to Dr. Roylott," Helen said. "It was enough money for all of us. The will also provided for my sister and me. When we married, we would each get a share of that 1,000 pounds.

"But Julia died two years ago at the age of 30. By then her hair had turned white from worry, just as mine has.

"Life was hard for us. Soon after we moved to Stoke Moran, Dr. Roylott began making enemies. Even today, he is making trouble with our neighbors. Most of the people in the village fear my stepfather because of his violent temper. His only friends are traveling gypsies. He lets them camp on his land."

Holmes nodded as he listened to her story. I could see that not a word was lost on him.

"Dr. Roylott collects animals from India," Helen continued. "He keeps a cheetah and a baboon on our estate. My home is not a pleasant place to live, believe me.

"Two years ago, Julia became engaged to a young man. Dr. Roylott offered no objections. But less than two weeks before the wedding, Julia died."

Holmes raised an eyebrow. "It is very important now that you give me all the details of her death," he explained.

The young woman thought for a moment, then said, "First, I should tell you more about Stoke Moran estate. The house is very old. The bedrooms are side by side on the ground floor. The first is Dr. Roylott's. The next is Julia's. Even though she is dead, I still call it hers. The last bedroom is mine.

There are no connecting doors between any of the rooms. But each room opens onto the same hallway and looks out upon the front lawn."

Holmes nodded as he listened and said, "I understand."

"The night Julia died," Helen continued, "Dr. Roylott went to his bedroom early. He didn't go to bed right away, though. Julia said she smelled the smoke from his Indian cigar."

Holmes tipped his head to the side and said, "Interesting."

"Julia came to my room and asked, 'Have you ever heard whistling in the middle of the night?' I told her no. She then said she'd heard strange whistling sounds for the past two nights. We decided it must have come from the gypsies camped nearby. Julia went back to her room, and I heard her lock her door."

Holmes leaned forward, and I could tell his mind was hard at work.

"In the middle of the night," Helen continued, "I heard a scream. I rushed into the hall. I think I heard a whistle and a clanging sound. Then I heard Julia's door being unlocked. Julia stepped into the hallway. Her face was white with terror, and she fell to the floor. She was in great pain and her hands and legs shook. Her last words were, 'Oh, my God, Helen! It was the band! The speckled band!'

"Dr. Roylott came out of his bedroom, but it was too late. Julia was already dead."

"Are you sure you heard a whistle and a clang?" Holmes asked.

"I think so," Helen said. "But maybe it was just the wind and the creaking of the house."

"What did the police say?" Holmes asked.

"They were suspicious, at first, because of Dr. Roylott's bad reputation. But they noticed no trace of poison. And there were no bruises or cuts on her body. It was clear that no one could have gotten into her room. The door and window were locked from the inside."

"What do you think 'speckled band' means?" Holmes asked.

"Maybe a band of gypsies," Helen said. "I don't know for sure. That all happened two years ago. Now something new has come up."

"Please go on," Holmes said.

Helen took a deep breath. "A young man has proposed to me. Dr. Roylott doesn't oppose the wedding. After I told him of it, he began remodeling the house. The work started with my bedroom. Because of that, I have moved into Julia's bedroom.

"Last night I heard a whistling sound. It scared me so much I ran from the house. I went to the Crown Inn across from Stoke Moran and from there to London. Here I am, and that is my story."

"I think there is more to it," Holmes said. He took one of Julia's hands in his and pushed up her sleeve. There were bruises on her arm. "What about these?" he asked.

The young woman sighed. "It is true. Dr. Roylott is sometimes rough with me."

Holmes bit his lip. I could see he was trying to hide his anger.

"Very well," he said. "I would like to see Stoke Moran, but not when Dr. Roylott is at home."

"Yes," Helen said. "He will be away all day. I'll take the train back and wait for you to come this afternoon." With that, she hurried out of the room.

"Interesting," Holmes said. "You noted that she will get some of Roylott's money if she marries? Just as her sister would have if she had lived."

Before I could reply, there was a sharp banging at the door. A huge man in a top hat stormed in. His sunburnt face sneered at each of us. "Which of you is Holmes?" he shouted.

Holmes smiled. "I am. You must be Dr. Roylott."

"I followed my stepdaughter here. What did she tell you?" Roylott screamed.

Holmes smiled once more. "Today is a very nice day. Are you enjoying our London weather?"

"I've heard about you and your detective work. I don't want you pushing your way into my business," warned Roylott.

Roylott's face grew even redder. "I'm warning you," he shouted. "I'm a dangerous man!"

Roylott picked up our fireplace poker and suddenly bent it. Then he said, "Stay out of my way!" He left the room, slamming the door behind him.

Holmes listened to Roylott's footsteps going down the stairs. He smiled at me and said, "I'm not quite so large, but I have my own ways." Holmes then picked up the poker and with a quick movement unbent it. "I hope that he doesn't catch up with Miss Stoner.

"Watson," Holmes said, "let us get ready for a train ride to the country."

That afternoon we arrived at the train station at Leatherhead and took a carriage to Stoke Moran. The large house at Stoke Moran was made of gray stone. It sat on a hill in the middle of a private park that was surrounded by a wooden fence. The front of the house overlooked a big lawn. Scattered about the lawn were a great many bushes and trees.

Helen Stoner met us at the gate. "My stepfather has gone into town," she said. "We me him," said Holmes and warned her of her stepfather's unpleasant visit. "You must lock yourself up tonight," he told her. "If he gets violent, we will take you to a safe place. Is there someone you can stay with?"

"Yes," she said. "My aunt lives not far from here. I sometimes visit her and stay the night."

"Fine," Holmes said. "Now, would you kindly show us the house?"

First, Helen showed us the outside.

"Yours looks in good shape," Holmes said.

"I don't think it needs remodeling," Helen said. "I think that was just an excuse to get me to move into Julia's room. Would you like to see my room?"

"No, thank you," Holmes said. "But I do want to look inside Julia's room."

She took us to the room, and Holmes spent a great deal of time examining it. "With the doors and windows locked, it's safe," he said. "No one could get in here."

He looked at a rope hanging near the bed. "The rope rings a bell in the housekeeper's room," Helen said. "Dr. Roylott put it there a couple of years ago."

Holmes gave the bedpost a shake. "Interesting," he said. "The bed is bolted to the floor."

Then he looked at the ceiling. The hanging rope was tied to a hook. Next to the hook was a small ventilator. "Very strange," he said. "The rope isn't connected to anything except that hook."

He pointed to the ventilator. "The cigar smoke your sister smelled must have come through there. But why would anyone build a ventilator to go from one room to another?"

"I don't know," Helen said. "Dr. Roylott had it installed the same time he put in the bell rope."

A moment later, we visited Dr. Roylott's room. A large chair was pushed against the wall. The chair was placed directly below the ventilator that connected to Julia's bedroom. A large iron safe, with a bowl of milk on top of it, was next to the chair. "Does Dr. Roylott have a cat?" Holmes asked.

"No," Helen said. "Just his animals from India. He keeps a cheetah and a baboon on the grounds."

A small dog leash with a noose on the end was hanging next to Dr. Roylott's bed. Holmes looked it over, then turned to Helen. "I have seen enough," he said. "Now I must ask you to help me in a dangerous plan. When Dr. Roylott comes home, you must pretend you don't feel well. Excuse yourself, and go to Julia's room and wait. When Dr. Roylott goes to his room,open the ventilator between his and Julia's room. Signal us with a lamp. Then go to your own room and keep it locked."

She agreed, and Holmes and I left the house. We went to the Crown Inn, just across the way. After dinner, we went to our room and began our watch.

At eleven o'clock that night, a light appeared in Julia's window. "There is our signal," Holmes said.

We left the inn and hurried across to Stoke Moran. It was dark, and we moved carefully across the lawn. All of a sudden, something jumped out of a tree and ran past us. "My God, what was that?" I shouted.

"Just one of Dr. Roylott's little pets," Holmes said. "The baboon."

I shook in the darkness, hoping that the cheetah would not suddenly appear.

When we got to Julia's room, the shutters were open. We climbed in. Then we felt our way to the bed in the darkness. Holmes whispered in my ear. "We must sit in the dark and not make the smallest sound. Do not fall asleep. Your life may depend upon it."

I took out my pistol and sat down on the edge of the bed. Holmes had no pistol, only a thin, strong cane.

What a long night that was! I had no idea what to expect as we sat in the darkness waiting.

We could hear the church bell ring out the hours. Twelve o'clock. One o'clock. Two. Then, not long after the clock struck three, Holmes gripped my arm.

A little light appeared through the slots in the ventilator. Holmes stood up, struck a match, and began violently striking the bell rope with his cane.

"You see it, Watson?" he shouted!

I heard a low whistle, but saw nothing. It was too dark for me to see what Holmes was striking, but his face was pale and filled with horror.

Suddenly, we heard a scream in the next room.

"Have your pistol ready!" Holmes said. He lit his lamp, and we rushed to Dr. Roylott's room.

The door was unlocked. The first thing I saw was the safe. Its door was open wide. Then I saw Dr. Roylott sitting in a chair. His eyes were open, but there was no life behind them. The dog leash lay across his lap. Around his head was a strange yellow band with brown speckles. "The band! The speckled band!" whispered Holmes.

Suddenly, the band moved. It was a snake!

"It's a swamp adder!" announced Holmes. "The deadliest snake in India."

He threw the noose of the dog leash around the snake's head. With a quick movement, he yanked it tight. Then he carried the snake at arm's length from the milk bowl to the safe. He threw the snake and leash into the safe and slammed the door shut.

After we called the police, we sent Helen to stay with her aunt for the night.

Before the sun came up, we were on our way back to London. Holmes was quiet until the train left the station. Then he began to talk. "The words 'speckled band' had me fooled for a while," he said. " I thought it meant a band of gypsies. But once I saw Julia's room, it became clear.

"The rope was there for a reason, but not to ring a bell. The bed could not be moved. Why? Simple. The rope had to be a bridge for whatever came through the ventilator from Roylott's room. He put the ventilator and the rope in the room two years ago. That was right after Julia announced she was getting married.

"I knew Dr. Roylott got animals from India, and I guessed the unwelcome visitor was a deadly snake.

The dog leash was to catch the snake. The milk in the room was to train it."

I shook my head. As always, I was amazed at the brilliant mind of Sherlock Holmes.

He pointed to the heavy chair pushed against the wall. "Dr. Roylott stood on this to hold the snake up to the ventilator.

"The whistle," he said, "was to call the snake back to his room. The clanging she heard was the safe door closing. For several nights in a row he stood on the chair to put the snake through the ventilator. He knew that sooner or later the snake would bite Helen. No one would notice two tiny bite marks.

"When I heard the snake hiss," Holmes said, "I attacked the rope."

"And drove it back through the ventilator," I said.

"Yes," Holmes said, "and caused it to turn on its master. I am partly to blame for Dr. Roylott's death, but I cannot say it weighs very heavily upon my conscience."

The Adventure of the Man with the Twisted Lip

Late one Friday night in June of 1889, I found myself in Upper Swandam Lane, standing outside a filthy old building. Isa Whitney was inside. He had not been home for two days. His poor wife thought I could find him at the Bar of Gold. It was a disgusting and dangerous opium den on the lower floor of the building. My task was to bring him home safely.

The building sits on the river bank, just east of London Bridge. I told my carriage driver to wait for me. Then I entered a long, low room, which was thick and heavy with brown opium smoke. In the gloom I could catch a glimpse of many men. They lay in strange poses. Their shoulders were bowed, their knees bent, their heads thrown back.

On a three-legged wooden stool sat a thin old man. His jaw rested upon his two fists, his elbows upon his knees. He stared into the fire.

The den's attendant approached me. "Do you want a pipe of opium?" he asked.

"No," I said, "I am here looking for Isa Whitney."

Just then I heard a cry and turned to see Whitney. His face was pale, and his hands were shaking.

"Oh, my!" he said, "It's Watson! I say, Watson, can you tell me what time it is?"

"Nearly eleven," I said.

"Of what day?"

"Friday."

"Good heavens! I thought it was Wednesday," sobbed Whitney.

"Your wife has been waiting two days for you. You should be ashamed of yourself!" I said.

"I am, Watson. I never planned to be here so long. Oh, poor Kate! I know how worried she must be."

I took Whitney's arm, and we headed for the door. As I passed the old man on the stool, he pulled at my coat. He whispered, "Walk past me. Then look back."

I knew the voice at once, even though it came from a stranger. The old man turned his head so that no one else could see him. Suddenly, he was changed into my good friend Sherlock Holmes! Then, in the blink of an eye, he looked like an old man again.

"Holmes! What are you doing in this den?" I whispered.

"Get rid of your friend," he said. "I'll explain outside."

"I have a carriage waiting," I said.

"Send him home in it. I will join you then."

After I sent Whitney on his way, Holmes came out of the opium den. He was still disguised as an old man. We walked around the corner, and Holmes straightened up. He looked as fit and as healthy as ever.

"I hope you don't think I've become an opium user, Watson. The trail of an interesting case brought me to that place, Watson," Holmes explained. "I went in disguise because I have enemies there. Many men have gone into that place and have never been seen again. I fear this has happened to St. Clair."

He whistled, and a horse and carriage that had been waiting for him appeared. "Can you join me in this case?" Holmes asked.

"If I can be of use," I answered.

"A trusty friend is always of use," said Holmes. "We'll be sharing a room at Mr. St. Clair's house in the village of Lee in Kent."

He did not have to ask twice. As we rode to Lee, Holmes filled me in on the details of the case.

"Some years ago," he began, "Neville St. Clair moved to Lee. He bought a large house there. He soon made many friends and married the daughter of a local brewer. They now have two children. St. Clair has no job, but he has investments in London. He goes there each weekday. He is 37 and is considered a good husband and a loving father.

"Last Monday he went to London earlier than usual. He told his wife he would bring home building blocks for their son.

"His wife also had to go to London that same day. She lost her way and found herself in Upper Swandam Lane. Suddenly, she heard a cry. She looked up to a second-floor window and saw her husband. He waved, then disappeared as though he had been yanked out of the window by an unseen hand.

"She rushed to the building—the same one where our paths crossed earlier today. The owner wouldn't let her in. She ran off down the street with tears in her eyes. Luckily, she met an inspector and two policemen. She told them her story, and they all went back to the building.

"They found no one on the second floor except for Hugh Boone. He is a horribly ugly man who rents a room there. Both he and the owner swore that no one but Boone had been on the second floor that afternoon. Then Mrs. St. Clair noticed a box of toy building blocks on the floor. Under the bed, the police found Neville St. Clair's boots, socks, hat, and watch."

"But no trace of Mr. St. Clair himself?" I asked.

"None, Watson," Holmes said. "A window in the room looked out over the river. The police found drops of blood on the windowsill. They believe someone may have killed St. Clair and thrown him into the river.

"The owner had been at the door when Mrs. St. Clair first tried to enter. He could not have been the cause of the crime. But Hugh Boone could have done it. He can't explain why Neville St. Clair's clothes were hidden in his room. The police took him to the station, where he is now being held.

"I have seen him before. He is a professional beggar. To avoid the police regulations, he pretends to sell matches. He has bright red hair and a face marked by a horrible scar. It makes his lip twist upward. I've watched him beg, and between his shocking appearance and his funny comments to passers-by, he takes in a lot of money.

"Boone was arrested and the police searched the river near the building. The tide was out, and they found St. Clair's coat. The pockets were filled with coins. They believe Boone threw St. Clair out the window. They think he then weighted the coat with coins and threw it out. He didn't have time to get rid of the other clothes, so he hid them under the bed."

"It certainly sounds possible," I said.

"Boone has a police record as a professional beggar," Holmes said. "But he has never been known to cause any serious trouble. I must say, Watson, this case looks so simple and yet is so difficult."

Before I could answer, Holmes tapped the carriage driver on the shoulder. "Turn in here," he said, pointing to a large house. It was the St. Clair home.

A moment later we were met by Mrs. St. Clair. "Any

good news?" she asked Holmes.

"No, but no bad news, either," he replied.

"Thank goodness for that," she said. "But come in. You must be weary from your long day." She showed us in.

"Now," she said, "I must ask a question. I am stronger than I look, so please be honest with me. Do you think Neville is still alive?"

Sherlock Holmes seemed embarrassed. "Frankly, madam," he said, "I do not."

"You think that he is dead?"

"I do," Holmes replied.

"On what day did he meet his death?"

"On Monday."

"Then how do you explain this letter I received from him today?" she asked.

Sherlock Holmes jumped up and said, "What?!"

"Yes, today." She held up an envelope. "He also sent his ring."

"May I see the letter?" Holmes said.

"Certainly," she replied.

He took the envelope and examined it closely. It was stamped with the Gravesend postmark and with that day's date.

"Surely this coarse writing is not your husband's, madam," Holmes said.

"No, but the letter is in his writing," she said. "And the ring is his."

Holmes read the letter aloud:

"Dearest, do not be frightened." "All will be well. There is a huge error which may take some little time to correct. Wait in patience.

Neville

"It is postmarked today," Holmes said. "But it may have been written on Monday and mailed later." He paused a moment in thought. "Tell me something," he continued, "When you saw your husband in Upper Swandam Lane, was he in ordinary clothes?"

"Yes, but he had no coat or tie."

Holmes smiled. "Then things may not be as dark as they look. We shall now have a little supper. Then we should go to bed, for we have a busy day tomorrow."

I was pleased to go to bed soon after we dined. Holmes, though, was too involved in finding an answer to the riddle to feel sleepy. He could go for days without rest. He would look at a case from every point of view.

He arranged five pillows on the floor and sat down on them cross-legged. He set an ounce of shag tobacco and a box of matches in front of him. The blue smoke curled up from his pipe. He sat motionless, deep in thought.

I fell asleep almost immediately. Near dawn Holmes shook me awake.

"Get dressed, Watson. We're headed for London.

The stable boy has a carriage ready."

He chuckled. "I think, Watson, that you stand in the presence of one of the biggest fools in Europe. But I may have the key to the affair now. It's in this little bag. Let us see if it fits the lock."

A few minutes later we were on the road to London. A few hours after that we entered the Bow Street Police Station. We went directly to the office of Inspector Bradstreet, whom Holmes knew well.

"Good morning, Inspector Bradstreet," Holmes said. "I'm here about Hugh Boone."

"Yes, Mr. Holmes," the inspector said. "We have him locked up."

"How is he behaving?" Holmes asked.

"Oh, he gives us no trouble. But he is a very dirty rascal."

"Dirty?" Holmes said.

"Yes. It is all we can do to make him wash his hands," said the inspector. "Well, he will soon be getting a regular prison bath. When you see him, I think you will agree that he needs it."

Bradstreet led us to the jail cells and opened a panel on one of the doors. "Here he is," Bradstreet said. "He's asleep, but you can see him very well."

The prisoner lay with his face toward us. He was in a deep sleep. He was a middle-sized man, poorly dressed, and as dirty as the inspector had said. And he was ugly. A scar ran from one eye down to his chin, making his lip twist upward. His hair was bright red.

"I had an idea he would need a wash," Holmes said. "I took this from the bathroom at the St. Clair home in Lee." He opened the bag as he spoke and took out a large bath sponge.

The inspector chuckled.

"Please open the door," Holmes said quietly. "We will make him look more respectable."

The inspector slipped his key into the lock, and we entered the cell. The sleeper turned, then settled down again. Holmes stooped to the water jug. He wet the bath sponge, then rubbed it firmly across the man's face.

He stepped back and spoke in a loud voice. "Let me introduce you to Mr. Neville St. Clair, of Lee, in the county of Kent!"

Never in my life have I seen such a sight! The man's face peeled off under the sponge like the bark from a tree. Gone was the coarse brown tint. Gone was the twisted lip. Off came the red wig! There, sitting up, was a pale, refined-looking man. He had black hair and smooth, healthy skin. He rubbed his eyes and looked about him, still half-asleep.

"It's the missing man!" Bradstreet shouted. "I know him from the photograph."

"All right," the prisoner said, "that's who I am. But what, pray tell, am I charged with?"

The inspector shook his head. "Well, I guess I don't know. I have been 27 years on the force, but this really takes the cake."

"If I am Mr. Neville St. Clair, no crime has been committed," the prisoner said. "You are holding me illegally."

"No crime, but a very great error has been committed," said Holmes.

"I was just trying to protect my family," groaned St. Clair. "I do not want my children to be ashamed of their father. What can I do?"

Sherlock Holmes sat down beside him. "If you tell us the truth," he said, "I believe we can keep it quiet."

"Oh, bless you!" cried the prisoner. "I would have even faced hanging, rather than let this secret hurt my family."

Then Neville St. Clair began to tell us his incredible story:

As a young man, I had worked as an actor in the theater. Later, I became a newspaper reporter in London. One day, my editor assigned me to do a story about beggars.

To understand the life of a beggar, I used my skills as an actor. I disguised myself as a beggar. At the end of the day, I had taken in more than 26 shillings. I was surprised. Five days of begging would bring in more than six-and-a-half pounds a week. As a newspaper reporter, I made only two pounds a week!

Not long after that, I found myself in need of 25 pounds. I took a leave of absence from the paper and went begging. In ten days I had the money I needed. I went back to reporting, but not for long. There was a fight between my pride and easy money. The money won. I quit my job and became a full-time beggar.

Only the landlord of the opium den knew my secret. There, I rented a room for changing into and out of my beggar disguise.

Before long I was wealthy. I earned more than 700 pounds a year. I bought a house in the country, married, and had children. But I continued to lead two lives. My wife and friends thought I had business interests in London. None guessed my true business.

Then my wife saw me in the second-floor window! I didn't know what to do. I tried to cover my face. Then I rushed to the owner of the place and told him not to let my wife in.

I went back to the room and put on my disguise. In my rush to get rid of my clothes, I cut my hand. I filled my coat pocket with coins to make it sink and threw the coat into the river. When I heard footsteps on the stairs, I hid the rest of my clothes under my bed."

"That's quite a story," Holmes said.

St. Clair spread his hands wide. "The rest you know," he said. "I sent my wife the ring and the note to keep her from worrying. I wrote it while the police were searching the house and slipped it to the

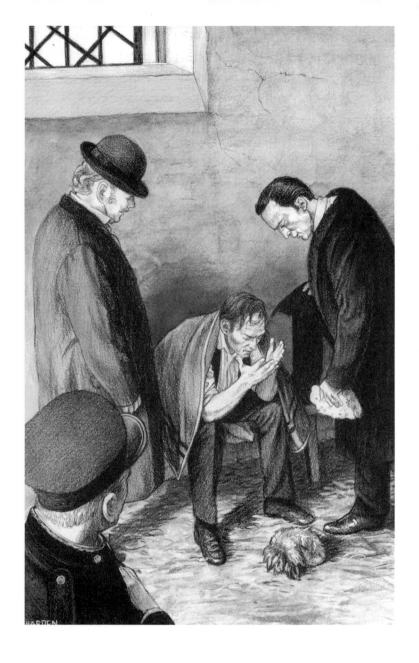

26

owner of the place."

"It only reached her yesterday," Holmes said.

"What a week she must have spent!" St. Clair said.

I said, "The owner must have thought the police were watching him. He probably gave the letter to someone to mail for him, and the person must have forgotten it for several days."

"That's probably the case," Holmes said. He turned to St. Clair. "Have you ever been arrested for begging?"

"Many times; but what was a fine to me?" answered St. Clair.

"But it must stop here," said Bradstreet. "If the police are to hush this thing up, there must be no more of Hugh Boone."

"I've learned a hard lesson," said St. Clair. "I swear I shall never work at begging again."

"Then no further steps need be taken." Bradstreet said. "But if we ever catch you again, it will all become public knowledge."

The inspector turned to Sherlock Holmes. "Thanks to you," he said, "this matter is solved. But I wish I knew how you reached your results."

"I reached this one," said Holmes, "by sitting on five pillows and smoking an ounce of loose tobacco."

He turned to me. "Now, Watson," he said, "let us leave for Baker Street. I think we can get there just in time for breakfast."

The Adventure of the Blue Carbuncle

Two days after Christmas, I visited Sherlock Holmes at 221B Baker Street.

The detective was in his purple dressing gown and had a serious look on his face. A battered old felt hat was on a nearby table. Next to it lay a magnifying glass.

"If you're busy," I said, "I can come back later."

"Not at all," Holmes replied. "I am glad to have a friend to talk with." He nodded toward the hat. "This is a small matter, but an interesting one."

"Is that a clue in some terrible crime?" I said.

Holmes laughed. "There is no crime. Just one of those funny events that happen in a large city."

"Tell me more," I said.

"Early Christmas morning, my friend Peterson the delivery man, was walking home from the police station. He saw a man carrying a white goose over his shoulder. Peterson was at the corner of Goodge Street. Suddenly, a gang of men attacked the man with the goose. The man fought back, and his hat went flying. He swung his cane at one of the men and broke a shop window.

"Peterson, helpful as usual, rushed to the man's

aid. However, Peterson's uniform must have scared the man, who probably thought Peterson was a policeman. He dropped his goose and ran off. The gang fled the other way. Once it was over, Peterson ended up with a Christmas goose and an old hat."

"And he had no way to return them?" I said.

"None," said Holmes. "The words 'for Mrs. Henry Baker' were written on a card tied to the bird's leg. The letters 'H.B.' were inside the hat. But there are hundreds of Henry Bakers in London."

"What did Peterson do?" I asked.

"He brought the hat and goose here and asked for my help. He took back the goose today, since it wouldn't keep. I think his wife is roasting it right now."

"Has Henry Baker put an ad in the paper?" I asked.

"No. But his hat offered some clues," Holmes replied.

"You're joking. What can the hat tell you?" I asked.

"Here, take my magnifying glass," Holmes directed. "You know my methods. Examine the hat closely."

I examined the hat carefully. Inside were those initials "H.B." Someone had put ink over a few faded places. "I can see nothing," I said, handing it back to my friend.

"Oh no, you see everything," Holmes said, "but

you don't think about what you see." He gazed at the hat. "I would say the owner was intelligent and was once wealthy. In the last three years, things have not gone well. I believe his wife no longer loves him."

"What?" I asked.

"He still has some self-respect," Holmes said. "He leads a quiet life and has gray hair, which he recently had cut. And he uses lime hair cream."

"Are you joking?" I said.

"Not at all," Holmes said. "First, the hat is large. That suggests a large head and large brain. He is probably intelligent. The hat is of good quality, but at least three years out of style. He could afford a good hat then, but he has not bought a new one. His finances must be in question."

"Well," I said, "what about his self-respect?"

Holmes pointed to a spot on the hat. "Here he used ink to cover up a discolored place. As bad as things are now, he still wants to look nice."

"Amazing!" I said.

"And, of course, I detected newly cut gray hairs in the hat and the smell of lime hair cream."

I shook my head. "It all fits. But surely you can't know that his wife doesn't love him."

"The hat has not been brushed for weeks," Holmes said. "When *your* wife lets you go out in such a state, I will know she no longer loves you."

"But he might be a bachelor," I suggested.

"No. He was bringing home the goose as a peace offering to his wife," Holmes replied.

I shook my head in wonder. "But there has been no crime, and no real harm done. Isn't this all a waste of energy?"

Just then the door flew open, and Peterson rushed in. "The goose, Mr. Holmes!" he said. "See what my wife found in its crop!" He held out his hand. In it was a beautiful blue carbuncle.

"Peterson!" Holmes cried. "Do you know what this is?"

"A diamond, sir? A precious stone?" answered Peterson.

"It is *the* precious stone man! The blue carbuncle! This was stolen from the Countess of Morcar. Its value can only be guessed. The reward is 1,000 pounds!"

"1,000 pounds!" Peterson dropped into a chair and shook his head.

"Didn't the robbery take place at the Hotel Cosmopolitan?" I asked.

"Yes," Holmes said. "Just five days ago. John Horner, a plumber, was accused of taking the gem from the lady's jewel box. The evidence against him is strong. He is being held in jail awaiting trial."

Holmes went to his files and took out a newspaper clipping. "Listen to this account," he said. Then he

began to read:

John Horner, 26, plumber, was accused of stealing a valuable gem from the Countess of Morcar. The gem, known as the Blue Carbuncle, was taken from her room.

Police questioned James Ryder, an attendant at the hotel. Ryder said he took Horner to the room on the day of the robbery to do repair work. Ryder said he left the room briefly. When he returned, Horner was gone. The jewel box had been broken open.

Horner was arrested, but the Blue Carbuncle was not found on him nor at his apartment.

Catherine Cusack, maid to the Countess, said she heard Ryder cry out. She rushed to the room, and Ryder showed her the broken jewel box.

Horner says he is innocent. Police records show he has been convicted of robbery once before.

Holmes put down the clipping. "Here's the question for us," he said. "How did the gem go from the jewel box to the crop of Peterson's goose? Here is the stone; the stone came from the goose; and the goose came from Mr. Henry Baker, a man with a bad hat. Perhaps he can fill in some gaps in our knowledge."

"How do we find him?" I said.

"We put an ad in the paper," Holmes replied. He picked up a pencil and paper and began to write.

"How does this sound?" he asked. "Found at the

corner of Goodge Street: a goose and a black felt hat. Mr. Henry Baker can have the same by calling at 6:30 this evening at 221B Baker Street."

"That is clear and to the point," I said. "Will he see the ad?"

"Such a loss is important to a poor man," Holmes said. "I believe he will check the ads."

Holmes handed the paper to Peterson. "Please have this placed in all the evening papers."

"And the gem?" Peterson asked.

"I shall keep it here," Holmes said. "And, Peterson, buy a goose on your way back. We need to give it to Mr. Baker to replace the one your wife is now cooking."

When Peterson left, Holmes held up the carbuncle. "A pretty thing," he said. "But of course it causes crime. Every great gem does. They are the devil's tools. Men have robbed, even killed to own this one."

"What will you do with it?" I asked.

"I'll lock it in my safe," Holmes said. "Then I'll drop a line to the Countess to say we have it."

"Do you think Horner is guilty?" I said.

"I don't know," said Holmes. "Maybe when we find Henry Baker, we will also find the truth."

That night, I visited Holmes again. At just about seven o'clock, a tall, heavy man also paid a visit. He had a wide forehead and an intelligent face. He wore an old black coat, but no hat.

"Mr. Henry Baker, I believe," said Holmes. "This is my friend Dr. Watson. Please take a chair."

"Thank you," said the man.

"Is this your hat, Mr. Baker?" Holmes said.

"Yes, sir, it is," said the man with a smile.

"I kept it in hopes of seeing an ad from you in the paper," Holmes said.

"I have been short of money lately," the man said. "I decided that the men who attacked me had carried off my hat and the bird. I didn't think there was a chance of getting them back."

"Of course," said Holmes. "By the way, we ate the bird."

"Ate it!" Baker leaped to his feet.

"It was going bad. But we have another one for you. It's the same size, and it's fresh."

"Oh, thank you," Baker said with relief.

"We still have the feathers, legs, crop, and so on of your own bird," Holmes said.

The man laughed. "What in the world would I do with them?"

Holmes nodded and said, "By the way, it was very tasty. Where did you get it?"

Baker said, "I often go to a local pub, the Alpha Inn. This year, the owner offered to sell us geese. We all put in a few pennies a week during the year. Then at Christmas, each person got a goose. The landlord at the inn gave us a good price."

"I see," Holmes said. A few moments later, he showed Baker out. Then Holmes said to me, "Mr. Baker knows nothing of the Blue Carbuncle. But I think I will follow up on a clue. Care to join me?"

"By all means," I said.

A short while later we entered the Alpha Inn. Holmes ordered two glasses of beer from the landlord. Then he said, "I hope your beer is as good as your geese."

"My geese?" the man said.

"Yes. Mr. Henry Baker, a member of your goose club, spoke highly of them."

"Oh, yes. But I don't raise them. I get them from Breckinridge at the Covent Garden Market," explained the landlord.

"Ah!" said Holmes.

We finished our beers and headed for the Covent Garden Market. We got there just as a man was rapidly closing the Breckinridge shop.

"Good evening," said Holmes. "Are you Mr. Breckinridge?"

The man nodded. "Yes," he said, "but I'm sold out of geese. Come back tomorrow."

"That's too bad," Holmes said. "I need one now. The landlord from the Alpha Inn sent us."

"Oh, yes, I sold him two dozen last week."

"Fine birds they were," Holmes said. "Where did

you get them?"

The man's face grew red with anger. "I'm getting tired of people asking questions about my geese! They're not the only geese in the world!"

"Well, I ask for a reason," Holmes said. "I bet five pounds the goose was from the country."

"You lose your bet," the man said. "It was raised in town."

"It couldn't have been," said Holmes. "All right, I'll bet you too. One sovereign?"

The man chuckled and took a black book from his pocket. "Now then," he said, opening his book, "here's a list of people I buy from. These are my town suppliers. Read that!"

"Mrs. Oakshott, 117 Brixton Road. December 22: 24 geese sold to Alpha Inn." Sherlock Holmes looked surprised. He took a sovereign from his pocket and gave it to the man. "You win," he said.

When we were out of sight of the store, Holmes laughed. "He looked like a gambler to me. If I offered to pay him to tell me, he wouldn't have. For only five shillings, we have the information we need."

Suddenly, we heard a shout around the corner. Breckinridge was yelling at a short, red-faced man. "Enough! I'll only talk about geese to Mrs. Oakshott, but I didn't buy any from you!"

"But one of them was mine all the same," the man shouted.

"Too bad," said Breckinridge. "Get out of here!"

The small man looked worried. He then turned and walked away from Breckinridge.

"Let's catch up with him," Holmes said. "This may save us a visit to Brixton Road."

A few minutes later, Holmes said to the man, "Excuse me. I think I can help you."

"Who are you?" the man said. "How can you help me?"

"My name is Sherlock Holmes. It is my business to know what other people don't know."

"But you can't know anything about this!"

"I know everything about it," Holmes said. "You are trying to find a goose that was sold to Mr. Breckinridge. He sold it to the landlord of the Alpha Inn, who passed it on to Mr. Henry Baker."

"Oh, sir," said the man, "you are the very person I wanted to meet!"

"We had better discuss it at my apartment," Holmes said. "Will you come with us?"

"Certainly," said the man.

"By the way, may I ask your name?"

The man looked away quickly. "My name is John Robinson," he said.

"No, no, your real name," Holmes said sweetly.

"All right. My real name is James Ryder."

Holmes nodded. "Right," he said. "And now, Mr. Ryder, let us go quickly. It will keep us warm."

When we got to Baker Street, Holmes said, "Now, you want to know about a white goose with black across its tail."

Ryder's eyes were wide. "Oh, yes!" he said. "Can you tell me where the goose went?"

"It came here," Holmes said. "I'm not surprised that you're interested in it." He went to his safe and took out the gem. "It laid an egg after it died—the prettiest blue egg!"

Ryder let out a gasp.

"The game is up, Ryder," said Holmes. "You are an attendant at the Hotel Cosmopolitan. An innocent man is in jail because of you. It will go easier for you if you tell me the truth now."

The man spoke in a weak voice. "It was Catherine Cusack who told me about the Blue Carbuncle."

"Yes," Holmes said, "the Countess's maid. And you knew that Horner, the plumber, had been convicted of robbery once before. You broke into the jewel box and took the gem. Then you and Catherine Cusack called in the police and blamed Horner."

Ryder dropped to his knees. "Please show mercy," he said. "This would break my mother's heart. I never went wrong before! I never will again. I swear it."

"Stand up!" shouted Holmes. "You want mercy? What about poor Horner?"

"I will leave the country," Ryder said. "Then there will be no witness to speak against Horner."

"We will talk about that later. First, tell me how the gem ended up inside the goose."

Ryder wet his lips. "When Horner was arrested, I got scared. I feared the police might search me and my room. I went to my sister's house."

"Mrs. Oakshott?" Holmes said.

"Yes," Ryder said. "She fattens geese for the market. As I walked through the backyard, I thought of a friend in Kilburn who is on the wrong side of the law. I thought he might sell the gem for me. But I still feared the police might find me and search me. Then I had an idea. My kind-hearted sister had promised me a goose for Christmas. I decided to feed the gem to the goose, then remove it when I butchered the bird. So I caught one and pushed the stone down its throat. It gave a gulp, and I felt the gem go into its crop. Just then my sister came out of the house, and the bird flew out of my arms to join the others.

" 'I've got your goose inside,' my sister said. I told her I'd already picked out the white one with the barred tail.

" 'Oh, very well.' she said. 'Kill it, and take it with you.'

"I did, and then I went to Kilburn, where I opened it and found no gem. I had the wrong goose!

"I rushed back to my sister's, but she had already sent the rest of the geese to Breckinridge. I went there and asked who had bought the geese.

Breckinridge said it was none of my business. I was asking again when you came along."

Ryder lowered his head and began to sob. "I am ruined! I have become a thief without ever seeing the money! What can I do!"

Holmes crossed the room and threw open the door. "Get out!" he said.

"Oh, Heaven bless you!" said Ryder.

"No more words. Get out!" ordered Holmes.

Ryder rushed out the door and down the stairs. We heard the front door bang shut.

"Watson," said Holmes, "I think the case is closed. I am not paid to handle the mistakes of the police. The important thing is, Horner is out of danger. Ryder will never testify against him. Perhaps I am committing a crime by not telling all. But I think Ryder has learned his lesson. He is far too frightened to turn to crime again. It would do no good to send him to jail."

Holmes took out his pipe and tapped it against the table. "Besides, Watson, Christmas is the season for forgiveness." He smiled at me and added, "Now let us go and have our dinner in which another goose will appear."

The Adventure of the Final Problem

It is with a heavy heart that I take up my pen. It is the last time I shall ever record the adventures of my friend Sherlock Holmes.

I did not wish to write about what happened two years ago. The events created a great emptiness in my life. But I have been forced to tell the story because of the letters that Colonel James Moriarty wrote to the newspapers. In them, he defended the memory of his evil brother. I have no choice but to tell what really took place between Professor Moriarty and Sherlock Holmes.

After my marriage, I did not see much of Holmes. Early in 1891, I heard he was working for the French government. Holmes sent me a note from France. He said he would be staying there for quite some time. But then, on April 4, 1891, my old friend appeared at my office. He looked paler and thinner than usual. He went to the window shutters and closed them.

"Are you afraid of something?" I asked.

"Of air guns, my dear Watson. You know I am not a nervous man. But I recognize danger when I am threatened."

Holmes held out his hand for me to see the cuts on

his knuckles. "The danger is solid enough for a man to break his hand over it," he explained. "Is your wife in?"

"She is away on a visit," I said.

"That makes it easier for me," he said. "Would you join me in a short trip to Europe?"

"Europe?" I said. "Where?"

"Oh, anywhere," he said.

It was not Holmes's nature to take an aimless holiday. Something was bothering him.

"Have you heard of Professor Moriarty?" Holmes asked.

"Never," I said.

"There you have the wonder of the thing!" he said. "His work can be seen everywhere, yet no one has heard of him. Watson, I want to beat that man. If I could free society of him, I should feel my career had reached its peak. I have enough money to retire now and live quite well, believe me. But I cannot rest so long as Moriarty is free."

"What has he done, then?" I asked.

"Moriarty's life has been a remarkable one," Holmes said. "He once was a university professor. He had a good career ahead of him. But he has a terrible criminal strain in his blood. Moriarty is all the more dangerous because he is so intelligent. He was forced to resign from his university position.

"There is no one who knows the criminal world of

London as well as I do," Holmes went on. "I have been aware of some power behind most of the crime that takes place here. It is a power that protects the criminals."

I raised an eyebrow.

"I have traced this power to ex-professor Moriarty," Holmes said. "He is the Napoleon of crime, Watson. Moriarty is the organizer of half that is evil and of nearly all that is undetected in this great city.

"He does little himself, but his agents are many. He plans robberies, burglaries—even murder. The agent may be caught, but never the planner. This was the organization I uncovered. I have devoted all my energy to breaking it up."

Holmes looked me in the eye. "Moriarty is the first enemy I have met who might be my equal. But he has made a mistake, and I may soon put an end to his evil. The net is ready to close. In three days, he and the top members of his gang will be arrested."

"But why are you going to Europe?" I asked.

"I must be careful that they don't learn of my plan," Holmes said. "Moriarty already suspects something."

"How do you know?" I asked.

Holmes smiled grimly. "I was sitting in my room this morning, thinking it over. The door opened, and Professor Moriarty stood before me.

"My nerves are strong, but I confess to being shocked at the sight of him. He is tall and thin, with a large forehead and sunken eyes. His head forever moves from side to side like a snake's.

"He stared at me. Then he said, 'It is dangerous to keep a loaded pistol in your pocket.' I did have one in my pocket," Holmes said. "I drew it out and laid it cocked upon the table.

"'You don't know me' Moriarty said.'"

"'Oh, but I do.' I said. "You have five minutes if you want to say anything."

"'You already know what I have to say,' said Moriarty."

"'Then you already know my answer. You want me to stay out of your business,' I said, 'but I cannot agree to that.'

"His face grew angry. 'You have interfered in my business at least five times in the last year. Now I may go to jail. You must drop it, Mr. Holmes. I would be sorry to have to kill you.'

"I stood up and said, 'Professor, our little talk is over. I have other business to attend to.'

"'Very well,' he said, 'but remember: Only one man will survive.' Then he turned and left."

"Do you think he will do you harm?" I said.

"He has already tried," Holmes said. "About noon, a horse almost ran me down. Not long after that, a brick fell from a building and nearly killed me. On the way here, a man with a club attacked me. I knocked him down, cutting my knuckles in the process. The police won't be able to connect him with Moriarty. But I know he is responsible."

"You're not safe on the streets," I said. "Why don't you spend the night here?"

"No, Watson," Holmes said. "I would be a dangerous guest. I'll leave by the back way. But I need to be away for several days until the trap closes on Moriarty and his gang. Will you join me?"

I agreed at once and listened as Holmes proposed a plan for our getting out of England.

The next morning I sent my luggage to Victoria Station with a messenger. Then I headed there myself by a roundabout way. Finally, I boarded the train. I went to the carriage that Holmes had instructed me to sit in. My bags were already there. However, Holmes was not. The time for the train to leave was drawing near. I was worried I would miss him. I was distracted for several moments as I helped an elderly Italian priest settle into one of the seats. The priest didn't speak much English.

Then the priest insisted on joining me in my compartment. I tried to tell him it was reserved for a friend. Finally, the train started to pull out of the station. I was gripped with fear. Had Holmes come to harm at the hands of Moriarty?

Then I heard a familiar voice. "My dear Watson,

you haven't even said good morning."

I turned in surprise. In an instant, the wrinkles were smoothed away from the old priest's face. His dull eyes were shining. The drooping figure sat erect. It was Holmes! Then his whole frame drooped again. Holmes had gone as quickly as he had come.

"How you startled me!" I cried.

"Sorry, Watson," Holmes said. "I had to be careful. I think they are hot upon our trail. Ah, there is Moriarty himself."

The train was moving as Holmes spoke. Glancing back, I saw a tall man pushing his way through the crowd. He waved his hand as though to stop the train. It was too late. We were rapidly gaining speed. Soon we were clear of the station.

"We barely made it," said Holmes, laughing. He took off the priest disguise and put the clothes in his bag.

"Have you seen today's paper?" Holmes asked.

"No," I answered.

"They set fire to my rooms last night, thinking I might be there. Moriarty must also have followed you to the station."

"I did exactly as you advised," I said.

Holmes smiled. "I'm sure you did, Watson. But now we must plan what we are to do about Moriarty."

"This train takes us directly to our boat

connection," I said. "I think we have escaped him."

"No," Holmes said. "He is too clever. He will hire a special train to follow ours. We will stop at Canterbury and wait. He is sure to catch up with us there."

"Let's have him arrested," I said.

"No, Watson," Holmes said. "It would ruin the work of three months. We would get the big fish, but the smaller ones would escape. On Monday, we will have them all.

"You and I will get out at Canterbury. We'll make a cross-country journey to Newhaven. From there we will cross by boat to Dieppe, France. Moriarty will continue on to Paris. He'll find our luggage there and wait for us to claim it. But we will get new luggage and take a roundabout trip to Switzerland."

The plan worked. We got off at Canterbury and waited for a carriage to Newhaven. We watched our train leave the station. Ten minutes later, a special train roared by. Holmes smiled. "That takes care of the Professor," he said.

On the following Monday, in Strasbourg, Germany, Holmes opened a newspaper. He let out a groan. "Moriarty has escaped! They caught the rest of the gang, but he is free. Watson, I think you had better return to England. I am in great danger now."

I told Holmes there was no chance I would leave him. So, for a week we wandered up the Valley of the

Rhone in Germany. From there we went to the Swiss Alps. The scenery was wonderful. But Holmes was not enjoying it completely. When we met new people, he checked their faces carefully. Once, on a mountain trail, a falling rock just missed us.

Our guide said rocks often fell at that spot. Holmes said nothing, but he smiled cautiously. I knew he suspected foul play. Yet for all his watchfulness he seemed happy. Several times he mentioned a wish of his: If he could free society from Moriarty, he would be happy to retire.

"I have spent much of my life solving crimes," he said. "Now I think I would like to spend time studying nature. Once Moriarty has been wiped out, I could end my own career."

And now I shall be brief in telling the rest of the story. It is not one I like to think about.

On May 3, we reached the little village of Meiringen in Switzerland. We took rooms at an English Inn, where our landlord spoke excellent English. He suggested we might enjoy a hike to the Reichenbach Falls nearby.

He was right. What a beautiful and fearful place it was! The flow of water, swollen by the melting snow, plunged into a deep abyss. The spray rises up like smoke from a burning house.

We stood on a ledge and looked down at the water as it hit the rocks far below us. The noise of the falling water was deafening.

As we stared at the breathtaking sight, a lad ran up the narrow path to the falls. He was carrying a note for me from our landlord. One of the guests at the inn was suffering an attack of some kind. The landlord knew I was a doctor and wondered if I could possibly help her.

It was impossible for me to refuse the request. Holmes said he wanted to spend more time at the falls. He urged me to go back to the inn, saying he would join me later.

On the way down the path, I glanced back at Holmes. He stood with his back against a rock and his arms folded. He stared down at the rush of the waters. It was the last that I was to see of him in this world.

When I was near the bottom of the slope, I looked back. I could see a man walking quickly up the narrow path I had just left. I didn't think much about him. My main concern was the ill woman.

At the inn, to my surprise, I found there was no such woman. "But what about this?" I said, showing the note to the landlord.

"I did not write it," he said. "Perhaps it was written by the tall, thin Englishman. He came in after you had gone."

I did not wait to hear more. I turned around and raced back toward the Reichenbach Falls.

When I returned to the falls, I found all that was left was Holmes's walking stick. It was still leaning against the rock where I last saw him. There was no sign of him. As I shouted, all I could hear was the echo of my own voice.

I knew what had happened. Holmes had waited on that narrow path. There was a steep wall on one side and a deep drop on the other. Then his enemy Moriarty had overtaken him. Two lines of foot-prints were clearly marked along the farther end of the path. Both led away from me toward the ledge. There were none returning.

I looked over at Holmes's walking stick. Something bright caught my eye. Lying on the ground by the stick was Holmes's silver cigarette case. Under it were a few sheets of paper. I saw that the handwriting belonged to my friend.

My dear Watson, the note said, I write these few lines through the courtesy of Mr. Moriarty. He and I shall soon settle some business that has long occupied us both.

Moriarty has told me how he avoided the English police. Also, how he kept track of our movements. He is indeed a very clever man.

I am pleased to think I shall soon free society from his presence. But I fear the cost will give pain to my friends, especially, my dear Watson, to you. I have already told you I would gladly end my career if I could rid the world of Moriarty.

I confess I knew the note about the ill woman was a trick. I did not want you involved in this business with Moriarty. I, and I alone, must finish it.

Tell Inspector Patterson that the papers he needs to convict the gang are in my desk in an envelope marked 'Moriarty.'

Please give my greetings to Mrs. Watson, and believe me to be, my dear fellow,

Very sincerely yours,
Sherlock Holmes

There is little more to say. The Swiss authorities examined the area near the ledge. They reached the same conclusion I had. Two men had fought, and both had gone over the edge. Two bodies were lost forever in that abyss. One was the most dangerous criminal of his time. The other was the foremost fighter for law and justice.

As to the gang, its members are behind bars. At the trial, little was said of their leader. That is one reason I have recorded this sad story. I want the world to know the truth about the master criminal, Professor Moriarty.

More important, I hope to preserve the memory of Sherlock Holmes. I regard him as the best and wisest man I have ever known.

53

The Adventure of the Empty House

In the spring of 1894, all of London was talking about the mysterious murder of Ronald Adair.

The case made me think of my old friend Sherlock Holmes. I wondered how he might have solved the crime. Again and again, I turned the case over in my mind. Still, I could find no reasonable solution to it. I realized again what a loss Sherlock Holmes's death had been to our country.

The newspapers called the case the Park Lane Mystery. It was the kind of case that would have interested Holmes.

Ronald Adair had lived with his mother and sister at 427 Park Lane. He had moved in the best society and had had no known enemies. He had belonged to several card clubs. The night he was murdered, he had played Whist at the Bagatelle card club. The other players had been Mr. James Murray, Sir John Hardy, and Colonel Sebastian Moran.

Adair had not often played for high stakes. But a week before his death, he and Colonel Moran had played as partners. They had done quite well. They had won 420 pounds from Godfrey Milner and Lord Balmoral.

The night of the crime, Adair had returned from his club at ten and gone to his room. At eleven-twenty, his mother had gone to his room to say good night. She had knocked on his locked door several times. Adair hadn't answered. Finally she had a servant force the door open.

The unfortunate young man was lying near the table. His head had been horribly injured by an expanding bullet. No weapon of any sort was found in the room, and no sound had been heard. There was a 20-foot drop beneath Adair's window. The police could find no footprints outside.

Money was stacked on the table next to a paper. The paper was a list of some of Adair's friends.

One evening, a few days after the crime, I visited Adair's home on Park Lane. A crowd of curious people had gathered there. Several of them had their own ideas of what had happened. All of their ideas seemed absurd.

As I was leaving, I bumped into an elderly man who was carrying a stack of books. I apologized, but the white-haired old fellow just snarled at me and turned away.

A few minutes after I got home, my maid came to my room. She said someone had come to see me. To my astonishment, it was none other than the unpleasant old book collector.

"Are you surprised to see me, sir?" he asked.

I said that I was.

"Well, I thought I had been a little rude to you," he said. "I came to apologize."

He pointed at my bookshelf. "I see you have an empty space there. Perhaps you would like to buy a book from me to fill it."

I looked at the shelf, then back at the man. There, to my amazement, stood Sherlock Holmes!

I think I must have fainted. The next thing I knew, Holmes was bending over me.

"My dear Watson," he said, "I owe you a thousand apologies. I had no idea you would be so affected."

I gripped him by the arms. "Holmes!" I cried. "Is it really you? Is it possible that you succeeded in climbing out of Reichenbach Falls?"

Holmes smiled. "I had no difficulty in getting out of the falls. The explanation is very simple. I never was in them."

"You never were in them?" I asked in disbelief.

"No, Watson, never. My note to you was absolutely genuine. I had little doubt that I had come to the end of my career. Professor Moriarty allowed me time to write the note, and then the struggle began.

"Moriarty was very strong. When he dragged me to the ledge, I thought the end was near. He knew his own game was up. He only wanted to get even with me. He knew he would die, but he wanted to take me with him.

"I have some knowledge, however, of baritsu, the Japanese system of wrestling. I slipped through his grip. With a horrible scream, he went tumbling over the edge. He fell for a long way and struck a rock. Then he bounced off of it and into the water."

"But the tracks!" I cried. "I saw them, with my own eyes. Two sets of footprints went down the path, but none returned."

"That was my plan, Watson. Immediately after Moriarty's death, I realized he was not my only remaining enemy. There were at least three other dangerous men who had worked with him who also wanted me dead. If they thought I had died, they would relax their guard. I could then come after them.

"I stood up and examined the rocky wall behind me and saw a few small footholds. The cliff is high and steep, as you are aware, but I decided to risk the climb.

"I watched from a higher ledge while you read the note, Watson. But moments later a rock came tumbling down and just missed me. I looked up and saw another man. I realized then that Moriarty had not come alone.

"I took another path down the mountain and after much hardship escaped the country. A week later I found myself in Florence, Italy. I was fairly sure that no one knew what had become of me.

"I made contact with my brother, Mycroft. He supplied me with money. But it was important that you should think I was dead to make my death seem convincing.

"Several times during the past three years I started to write to you. But I feared your regard for me would tempt you to tell my secret. That's why I turned away from you tonight in Park Lane. If you had recognized me you might have cried out. I might have been recognized by my enemies. The course of events in London did not run so well as I had hoped. The trial of the Moriarty gang left two of its most dangerous members free.

"I traveled around the world, spending time in Tibet, Persia, and North Africa. I even spent time doing scientific research in the South of France.

"When I learned that only one of my enemies was in London, I planned my return. It was hastened by the news of this Park Lane Mystery.

"I came at once to London. I went to Baker Street and almost scared Mrs. Hudson to death. But she recovered. The good woman had left my rooms exactly as they had been left by me."

Holmes touched my arm. "I am sorry about your wife's death, Watson. Work is the best thing to do for you and I have important work tonight. I would be most pleased if you would join me."

He did not have to ask twice. What a pleasure to

work with my brilliant friend once more!

It was like old times when later that evening, I found myself seated beside him in a carriage. I had my pistol in my pocket and the thrill of adventure in my heart. I thought, at first, we were headed for Baker Street, but Holmes had the driver take us to Cavendish Square. We got out, and Holmes led me through back streets and alleys. Soon, I had no idea where we were.

At last we came to the back of a large house. Holmes took out a key and opened the door. It was very dark and empty. The floor creaked and crackled as we climbed the stairs. We entered a room with dusty windows that looked out on a street. A wisp of light from a street lamp worked its way through a smudge in the dust.

"Do you know where we are?" Holmes whispered.

"Why, it's Baker Street," I said, staring through the dim window.

"Exactly. We are across from our old quarters."

"Why are we here?" I asked.

"Look," he said, pointing to the front window of one of the rooms we had shared. The shade was down. Behind it I could see the shadow of a man. The face was turned half 'round. It looked exactly like Holmes!

"It was made by the sculptor Oscar Meunier, of Grenoble, France. I put it there this afternoon.

Mrs. Hudson, hiding from sight, moves it from time to time to make it seem real."

"You thought the rooms were watched?" I asked.

"Yes. When I glanced out of the window, I saw their spy. I knew he had been put there by Moriarty's friend. He is the man who dropped the rocks over the cliff. He is the most dangerous criminal in London now, and he is after me. What he doesn't know is that we are after *him*."

For hours, we waited by the window. At last, as midnight approached, Holmes gripped my arm. Suddenly, I was aware of a sound coming from downstairs. A door opened and shut. We heard footsteps on the stairs.

Holmes guided me into a corner of the room. A moment later the door opened. I saw the outline of a man. He passed close by us and went to the window, which he opened about six inches.

By the light from the street lamp we could see he was an elderly man. He had a long, thin nose. He was partly bald and had a large gray mustache. An opera hat was pushed to the back of his head, and he wore a tuxedo.

In his hand he carried what appeared to be a stick. But as he laid it down upon the floor, it gave a clang. It was a rifle! He pumped a lever on it that made a whooshing sound. Then he loaded the weapon and knelt by the window. Slowly he raised the rifle. He took aim at the figure in the window across the street.

His finger tightened on the trigger. There was a loud whiz. Then Holmes leaped like a tiger onto the man's back. He hurled the man flat upon his face. Quickly, Holmes handcuffed the man. Then he took a whistle from his pocket and blew on it loudly.

A moment later, three policemen rushed up the stairs. They ran into the room. One of them was Inspector Lestrade, whom Holmes knew well.

The policemen uncovered their lanterns, and we got a good look at our prisoner. He looked intelligent, but you could see cruelty in his cold blue eyes. Those eyes stared at Holmes's face with both hatred and amazement. "You fiend!" he said to Holmes. "You clever, clever fiend!"

"This, Watson, is Colonel Sebastian Moran, once of Her Majesty's Indian Army. He is one of the best big-game hunters in the world," said Holmes.

The fierce old man said nothing but glared at my companion. With his savage eyes and bristling mustache, he seemed like a tiger himself.

Holmes picked up the rifle and examined it. It was an air gun. "Quite a weapon," he said. "It makes little noise and has great power. It was made especially for the late Professor Moriarty. It shoots a very special bullet."

Lestrade told his men to take Colonel Moran to

the station. Then Lestrade announced, "We will charge him with the attempted murder of Mr. Sherlock Holmes."

"Not so, Lestrade," Holmes said. "I do not propose to appear in the matter at all. To you, and to you only, belongs the credit of this remarkable arrest. You have solved the Park Lane Mystery."

"What?" Lestrade said in astonishment.

Holmes smiled and said, "Colonel Sebastian Moran shot Ronald Adair with an expanding bullet from an air gun. He fired through the open window of the second-floor front window of No. 427 Park Lane. That's the charge, Lestrade."

Holmes turned to me. "Now Watson," he said, "let's go to our old rooms."

Everything was as I remembered it, but neater. Mrs. Hudson was waiting for us with the dummy.

"Well done, Mrs. Hudson," said Holmes.

"I'm afraid the bust is ruined," she said, "but here's the bullet."

"Thank you. It's a soft revolver bullet, Watson," Holmes said as he showed it to me. "Who would expect to find an expanding bullet fired from an air gun? It is a good example of the Colonel's criminal mind.

"Moran has quite a history, Watson," Holmes continued. "Have you heard of him?"

"No, I have not." I answered.

"Ah, well, you had not heard of Professor James Moriarty either, as I recall." He took a file from a cabinet Mrs. Hudson had recently dusted. On the cover of it was printed "Colonel Sebastian Moran." Below the name, Holmes had written, "The second most dangerous man in London."

I read the file with interest, then gave it back to Holmes. "This is astonishing," I said. "The man's career is that of an honorable soldier."

"It is true," Holmes answered. "Up to a certain point he did well. But somewhere along the line, he began to go wrong. Troubles arose, and he was forced to quit the army. Soon after that, Professor Moriarty brought him into his gang.

Holmes tipped his head to one side. "Remember the time I closed the shutters at your office for fear of air guns? I knew then that one of the best shots in the world was after me. It was he who tried to kill me with rock slides near Reichenbach Falls.

"The problem was, I never had proof of his crimes. But during my days in hiding, I read the papers carefully. I hoped he would make some fatal mistake. So long as he was free in London, my life would be worth nothing.

"Then came the death of Ronald Adair. As soon as I read he had played cards with Colonel Moran, I guessed who had killed him. No sounds were heard that night when the shot was fired. That told me that weapon had to be an air gun. By the way, the bullet he used can be connected to the air gun.

"I returned to London ready to bring Moran to justice. But one of his spies saw me, and the Colonel realized I was on to him. He knew he had to kill me."

"Why did he murder Ronald Adair?" I asked.

"Remember that Colonel Moran and Adair had been partners in a card game," Holmes said. "They won a lot of money. I believe Adair had discovered Moran was cheating and threatened to expose him. He had probably asked Moran to give up his club membership and not play cards again.

"That would mean ruin to Moran. He had made much of his living by cheating at cards. The night he had shot Adair, the young man had been figuring out how much money he owed to the people who had been cheated. He had locked the door to his room from the inside to keep his mother out."

I nodded. "Clearly you have hit upon the truth."

"It will be proved or disproved at the trial," Holmes said. "Meanwhile, Colonel Moran will trouble us no more."

"What about you?" I asked.

Holmes smiled. "London still seems to offer many problems and puzzles to be solved," he said. "Watson, I believe the time is ripe for Sherlock Holmes to come out of retirement."

The Adventure of the Priory School

One fine May morning, Thorneycroft Huxtable visited Sherlock Holmes and me. He was a large man. His heavy face was etched with lines of trouble. His chin was unshaven and his shirt quite wrinkled.

"I came myself," Huxtable said, "because I feared no telegram would convince you of the urgency of the case. You must come with me to Mackleton by the next train."

"I am sorry," Holmes said, "but I am very busy now. Only the most important matter could draw me away."

"Important!" our visitor said, "Have you not heard of the kidnapping of the Duke of Holdernesse's son?"

"What! The former Cabinet Minister?" asked Holmes.

"We had tried to keep it out of the papers," said Huxtable, "but I thought it might have reached you."

Holmes paused. "The Duke and his wife have a son, Arthur, who holds the title Lord Saltire."

"He is the one," said Huxtable. "The Duke has offered 5,000 pounds for finding him and 1,000 for the names of the kidnappers."

"It is a very generous offer," said Holmes. "Give us some information about the case."

Huxtable rubbed his chin and said, "Priory is a preparatory school. I am the founder and principal. Recently, the Duke of Holdernesse sent his secretary, Mr. James Wilder, to enroll Arthur in my school. He is ten and the Duke's only child.

"The Duke and his wife have separated. She now lives in France. The boy was miserable after she left, so the Duke sent him to my school.

"Arthur vanished from his second-floor room last Monday. His window was open, and there is an ivy plant leading to the ground. A suit and a pair of shoes are missing. There were no signs of a struggle.

"Mr. Heidegger, a teacher, is also missing. His room was next to Arthur's. We know Heidegger left partly dressed because his shirt and socks were on the floor. He climbed down the ivy and left footprints on the lawn. Oh, and his bicycle is missing.

"We went immediately to Holdernesse Hall, just a few miles from the school. The Duke is very worried. Mr. Holmes, if ever you used your great detective powers, I beg you to do so now."

"You should have come sooner," Holmes said.

"The Duke was afraid other family matters might come to light," answered Huxtable.

"Are the police involved?" Holmes asked.

"Yes, sir, but nothing has come of it."

"Well," Holmes said, "I shall look into it."

"Did anyone come to see the boy on the day before he disappeared?" Holmes asked.

"No," Huxtable said.

"Did he get any letters?" Holmes asked.

"Yes, one from his father," Huxtable said.

"I see. But none from France?"

"No, never," said Huxtable.

"Well," Holmes said, "either the boy was carried off by force or he went of his own free will. In that case, you would think someone from outside convinced him to flee. If he has had no visitors, the idea to leave must have come in the letter. Were he and his father very friendly?"

"His Grace is not very friendly with anyone," Huxtable admitted. "He was kind to the boy in his own way. But the boy's feelings were for his mother."

"Did he tell you that?" Holmes asked.

"No. His secretary told me."

Holmes nodded, then said, "If you will, please give us some time to pack."

We reached the school at dusk, and the Duke and James Wilder were waiting for us. The Duke was tall, with a pale face and a full red beard. James Wilder was shorter and smooth-faced.

Wilder said to Dr. Huxtable, "His Grace is surprised you contacted Mr. Holmes."

"But surely, Mr. Wilder—"

"His Grace wants to avoid scandal," said Wilder. "He prefers to let as few people as possible know about the matter."

"All right," said Dr. Huxtable. "Mr. Sherlock Holmes can return to London in the morning."

"Hardly," Holmes said. "This northern air is pleasant, so I plan to spend a few days here. Whether I stay here or in the village is up to you."

"I agree with Mr. Wilder," said the Duke to Huxtable. "But since Mr. Holmes is here, it would be foolish not to use his services. Mr. Holmes, I should be pleased to have you stay with me."

"I thank your Grace," said Holmes. "But I think it would be wiser to remain at the scene of the mystery."

"Just as you like," said the Duke. "Mr. Wilder or I will help you in any way possible."

"Have you had ransom demands?" asked Holmes.

"No, sir," the Duke replied.

"I understand that you wrote to your son the day this incident occurred," Holmes said.

"No, I wrote him the day before," said the Duke.

"Was there anything in your letter that might have made him take such a step?" asked Holmes.

The Duke frowned. "No, certainly not."

"Did you mail the letter yourself?" asked Holmes.

Wilder interrupted, "His Grace does not mail

letters himself. *I* put it in the mail bag."

Holmes nodded but said nothing.

"I advised the police to look in the South of France," said the Duke. "I do not believe my wife would encourage this act, but the lad had some odd opinions. He may have fled to her, helped by that teacher."

Holmes had no more questions. But after the Duke left, he went out for a while. He returned with a map of the area and laid it out on the table.

"Look at this," Holmes said. "The main road runs east and west by the school. There is no side road for a mile either way. If the boy and Heidegger went that way, they would have had to pass a policeman. He was on duty from twelve to six. I spoke with him tonight, and he saw no one. The other way on the road goes to the Red Bull Inn. Its landlord watched all night for a doctor. The doctor didn't come until morning. No one else came by.

"If they didn't go by road," Holmes said, "they had to go north or south. To the south, the land is cut up into many small farms. The stone fences would make a bicycle trip very unlikely.

"To the north is a grove of trees. Then there's a moor. On the other side of the moor is Holdernesse Hall. A few farmers raise sheep and cattle on the moor, and there is another inn farther along. There are paths, but no roads. Logic says they went north.

Tomorrow we'll investigate."

At the break of day, Holmes woke me. "Come," he said. "We have a big day ahead of us."

The moor was filled with little paths. We saw many sheep and cow tracks. There was no sign of the boy or Heidegger.

We came to a black ribbon of a path, and Holmes said, "Look here, Watson, a bicycle track, but not *the* bicycle. I know 42 different impressions left by tires. This is a Dunlop, with a patch on it. Heidegger's tires were Palmers."

Holmes leaned close to the track. "The hind wheel left a deeper impression than the front and has crossed it in several places. That tells me the rider was heading away from the school."

We followed the track until it was wiped out by cattle tracks. Back on the moor Holmes spied another bicycle track. "Palmer tires. And look, the rider fell here!"

The ground was disturbed, and there were a few footprints. Then the tracks resumed. Holmes held up a branch from a bush. To my horror, I saw stains of blood.

"Bad!" said Holmes. "See, the rider fell, was wounded, stood up, then continued on. But there is no other track. Cattle tracks on the side, but nothing else."

Suddenly, we noticed the bicycle. Blood was

smeared on the frame. Then, to our horror, we found the rider—dead. He was a tall, bearded man. The cause of his death was a blow to the head. He wore shoes but no socks. It was Heidegger.

"We should push on," Holmes said, "but we have to inform the police of the discovery."

Just then, we saw a fellow coming down the path. Holmes called him over and asked him to take a note to Huxtable. The man rushed off with it. He seemed happy to get away from the horrid sight.

"Watson," said Holmes, "the boy was fully dressed when he fled, so he had a plan. He was not in a hurry that would have forced him to leave wearing his nightclothes. But Heidegger left without his socks. I believe he saw the boy leave and went after him. Heidegger dressed in a hurry and set out on his bicycle. Five miles later, he met his death from a blow no young boy could deliver. There must have been someone else. How did they get so far before Heidegger caught up? We found no bicycle tracks or signs that they were on horseback."

"Holmes," I cried, "this is impossible!"

"We have solved worse problems. Now let's see what the Dunlop with the patch has to offer."

We found the Dunlop track again and followed it to a spot that might have led to Holdernesse Hall or to the village that lay in front of us on Chesterfield Road. There was an inn there. As we approached it,

Holmes let out a groan and grasped his ankle. He limped up to the inn door, where a man was smoking a clay pipe.

"Are you Reuben Hayes?" asked Holmes.

"How do you know my name?" the man asked.

"It's printed on the board above your head," Holmes said. "I hurt my ankle. I wonder if you have a carriage in your stables for rent."

"No, I have not," Hayes said.

"I will pay well for the use of a bicycle," said Holmes.

"Where do you want to go?" asked Hayes.

"To Holdernesse Hall," said Holmes.

"Pals of the Duke?" asked the landlord.

Holmes said, "He'll certainly welcome us."

"Why?" Hayes asked.

"We have news of his lost son," Holmes said.

The landlord gave a start. "You have?"

"The police think he is in Liverpool. They expect to find him soon," said the man.

The man's manner was suddenly pleasant. "I have no love for the Duke. I was his coachman, and he fired me. But I'm glad the lad has been found. I'll help you to take the news to the Hall."

"Thank you," said Holmes. "We'll have some food first. Then you can bring 'round the bicycle."

"I have none. I'll rent two horses to you," said Hayes.

"All right," said Holmes. "We'll talk about it after we've had something to eat."

As we were eating, Holmes said, "Watson, you saw cow tracks on the path. But did you see cows?"

"I don't remember seeing any," I replied.

"Strange," Holmes said. He arranged some bread crumbs on the table. "The cow tracks were sometimes like this, sometimes like that, and sometimes like this."

I wasn't sure what he meant.

"What kind of cow walks, canters, and gallops?" He stood up. "Let us visit the stables."

There were two dirty horses in the stable. Holmes raised the hind leg of one and laughed. "Old shoes, but new nails. Very interesting."

Suddenly, we heard a sound. Reuben Hayes stood behind us, a short, metal-headed stick in his hand. "What are you doing here?" he snarled.

"What's wrong?" asked Holmes, coolly. "Are you afraid we might find something?"

"I have nothing to hide," said Hayes.

"No harm then," said Holmes. "And forget the horses. I think we will walk."

We left, but we stopped just around the first curve. Holmes said, "We need another look." Then he started up the hill leading to the inn. Halfway up, he noticed a bicycle coming from the direction of Holdernesse Hall. We dropped flat to the ground.

The man flew past us, and I caught a glimpse of his face. It was James Wilder, the Duke's secretary! A minute later, from the hilltop, we saw his bicycle leaning against the wall by the inn's front door.

As darkness fell, we saw a carriage come from the stable. It hurried off in the direction of Chesterfield. "A single man in an open carriage," Holmes said. "But not James Wilder, for there he is!"

Wilder stood in the doorway of the inn. Then we heard footsteps, and another man appeared. The man followed Wilder back inside. About five minutes later, a lamp was lit in an upstairs room.

"Come," Holmes said, and he pulled me toward the inn. Once there, he struck a match and held it near the bicycle. The back tire was a patched Dunlop! Holmes looked up at the lighted window. "Give me a hand up, Watson." An instant later, his feet were on my shoulder. Just as quickly, he was down again.

"I think we have what we need," he said.

Holmes and I returned to the school. Then he went on to Mackleton Station to send telegrams.

At eleven o'clock the next morning, Holmes and I were met at Holdernesse Hall by James Wilder. He said in a cool tone, "I am sorry, but the Duke is far from well. He has taken to his bed."

"I will see him there," Holmes said. It was clear Holmes would not take no for an answer.

75

Wilder had told the truth. When we arrived at Holdernesse, the Duke looked sickly. Holmes greeted him, then said, "I can speak more freely in Mr. Wilder's absence."

Wilder glared at Holmes.

"All right," said the Duke. "Mr. Wilder, would you please step outside of the room for a moment?"

Wilder frowned again, but he left the room.

Then Holmes said, "I understand you have offered 5,000 pounds to anyone who will tell you where your son is. And you'll give another thousand for the name of the person responsible."

"That is true," said the Duke.

"I see your checkbook upon the table. Please write me a check for 6,000 pounds."

"That is not funny, Mr. Holmes," said the Duke.

"I was never more serious in my life," Holmes answered. "I know where your son is, and I know who is holding him."

"Where is he?" gasped the Duke.

"He is at the Fighting Cock Inn," said Holmes, "just two miles from here."

"Whom do you accuse?" said the Duke.

"I accuse you," said Holmes. "And now, your Grace, I'll trouble you for that check."

The Duke let his face fall into his hands. Finally, he said, "How much do you know?"

"I saw you together last night," Holmes replied.

The Duke picked up a pen and opened his checkbook. "If only you two know about this, there is no reason it should go any farther. I think 12,000 pounds is the sum I owe you."

Holmes said, "It cannot be handled so easily. There is Heidegger's death to be accounted for."

"James knew nothing of that," the Duke said. "It was the work of the brute he hired."

"When a man plans a crime," Holmes said, "he is morally guilty of any other crime that comes from it."

"Morally guilty, but a man cannot be blamed for a murder that he took no part in and that he despises. The instant he heard of it, he told me all. Oh, Mr. Holmes, you must save him!" cried the Duke.

"Perhaps," said Holmes. "But you must tell me the whole story. I realize that you want to protect James Wilder and that he is not the murderer."

"No, the murderer has escaped," said the Duke.

Holmes shook his head. "No, Reuben Hayes was arrested at Chesterfield last night."

The Duke showed surprise. "I am glad Hayes has been taken into custody. Will that affect my elder son?"

It was Holmes's turn to look shocked.

"I promised the truth," the Duke said. "James is my son by a lady I loved, but who would not marry me. When she died, I took him in. I could not claim him as a son. But I gave him an education and made him my personal secretary. He found out the truth of his birth and became angry and jealous of Arthur. I sent the lad to school to keep James from harming him.

"When James decided to kidnap Arthur, he hired Hayes to help him. James slipped a note into the letter I sent Arthur. It said his mother was waiting to see him. It told him to go to a grove near the school. A man would be there with a horse, and they could ride to meet his mother.

"The man with the horse was Hayes. On the way to the inn, Heidegger caught up with them, and Hayes killed him. James learned of it only yesterday."

"What were James's plans for the boy?" Holmes asked.

"He hoped to force me to change my will. He hoped that he, not Arthur, would inherit my estate. He knew I wouldn't go to the police. But when Heidegger's body was found, James was overcome with grief. He confessed and asked me not to say anything until Hayes could escape. I agreed, for I have always been weak with James.

"He went to the inn to warn Hayes. As soon as it was dark, I went there to see my dear Arthur. I agreed to leave him there for three days with Mrs. Hayes, a kind woman who was not part of the plan. I was wrong, but I wanted to protect James."

Holmes's face showed the anger he felt. "To

protect your guilty elder son," he told the Duke, "you have exposed your innocent younger son to great danger. I will help you, but you must immediately send a servant to bring Arthur home."

"Agreed," said the Duke. A moment later, a servant was on his way to the inn.

"It is possible," said Holmes, "that the facts need not be made public. As to Hayes, the gallows await him. But what about James Wilder?"

"He shall leave me forever and go to seek his fortune in Australia," the Duke said.

"Good," Holmes said. "Oh, by the way, did James Hayes use horseshoes that leave cattle tracks?"

The Duke looked surprised for a moment. "Come," the Duke said. Then he led us to a glass case in the next room that held strange-looking horseshoes.

"These were dug up near Holdernesse Hall. They were made for horses, but they were shaped with a cloven foot of iron in order to create cow tracks. They throw pursuers off the track."

Holmes opened the case and ran a finger along the shoe. A thin film of recent mud was left upon his skin.

"It is the second most interesting object that I have seen around here."

"And the first?" asked the Duke.

"I am a poor man," said Holmes, folding up the check from the Duke. He tucked it into his coat pocket and, with a smile, patted it fondly.

The Adventure of the Six Napoleons

Inspector Lestrade of Scotland Yard often visited Sherlock Holmes and me. The inspector usually let us know what was going on at police headquarters. In return for the news, Holmes gave him advice about cases.

One evening, Lestrade told Holmes the police were working on a very odd case. "It is a small matter. Still, I know you have a taste for the extraordinary."

"Tell me about it," urged Holmes.

"Someone hates Napoleon so much, he is going around London breaking statues of him. And he commits burglary to get at them," said Lestrade.

"Very interesting," Holmes said. "Let me hear the details."

"The first case occurred four days ago at the art shop of Mr. Morse Hudson on Kennington Road. Hudson was in the back of his shop and heard a noise. He rushed out to the front room and found a plaster bust of Napoleon smashed to pieces. Whoever had done it was gone.

"A more serious case involved a Dr. Barnicot of Kensington. He had two busts of Napoleon he had bought from Hudson. He kept one at home and the other at his office on Lower Brixton. Last night, a thief broke into his house and his office. Both busts were smashed.

"Strange," said Holmes. "Were the two busts the same as the one smashed in Morse Hudson's shop?"

"They all came from the same mold," said Lestrade.

"Then the man does not have a general hatred of Napoleon," said Holmes. "There are hundreds of statues of Napoleon in London. He only smashes one kind. This crime is too carefully planned to be the act of a madman."

"What do you mean?" I asked.

"In Dr. Barnicot's house," Holmes said, "a sound might wake the family. The thief was careful enough not to wake anyone. Lestrade, the case interests me. Please keep me up to date on it."

The next morning, Holmes read a telegram to me. It said, "Come to 131 Pitt Street, Kensington, at once." It was from Inspector Lestrade.

"I suspect it involves one of the statues," Holmes said. "Will you join me?"

A bit later we reached a small house on Pitt Street. Lestrade greeted us and introduced us to a man in a bathrobe. He was Horace Harker of the *Central Press* newspaper.

"It's the Napoleon bust business again," said

Lestrade. "The affair has taken a serious turn."

"What has it turned to, then?" Holmes asked.

"To murder," said Lestrade. "Mr. Harker will explain."

Harker said, "All my life I have been reporting news about other people. Now something has happened to me, and I'm confused. I can barely put two words together. But I'll try."

Holmes sat down and listened.

"I bought a bust of Napoleon four months ago from the Harding Brothers shop," Harker said. "At about three o'clock this morning, I was awakened by a horrible scream. I went downstairs and saw a window wide open. The bust was missing.

"I opened my front door and almost fell over a dead man. He lay on his back with his throat cut. I immediately called the police."

"Who was he?" asked Holmes.

"We don't know," Lestrade said. "He is tall, sunburned, and not more than 30 years of age. A horn-handled knife was lying in a pool of blood beside him. There was nothing in his pockets except a small map of London and a photograph. Here it is."

The photograph showed a sharp-featured man with thick eyebrows and a big jaw.

"What became of the bust?" asked Holmes.

"It was found in the front yard of an empty house near here," said Lestrade. "The bust was smashed to pieces. Come, I'll show you."

When we reached the yard, Holmes picked up several of the pieces and examined them carefully. "Imagine, this cheap bust was worth more, in the criminal's eyes, than a human life."

He pointed to the street lamp above our heads. "He chose a place where he could not be heard, and where he could have light."

"Dr. Barnicot's bust was broken near his lamp," Lestrade said.

"What is your next step?" Holmes asked.

"First, we must identify the dead man," Lestrade said. "His friends may lead us to the murderer."

"You follow your line, and I'll follow mine. We can compare notes later," replied Holmes.

"Very good," said Lestrade.

"Please tell Harker that I believe a madman did it. He can use it in his article," Holmes said.

Lestrade stared. "You think so?"

Holmes smiled. "I am sure it will interest his readers. By the way, Lestrade, could you meet us at Baker Street at six this evening? Until then I should like to keep this photograph."

A short while later, Holmes and I went to Morse Hudson's art shop. Hudson was a heavy man with a red face. "The man came right into the shop and smashed it! Disgraceful, sir, that's what it is!" exclaimed Hudson.

Hudson had bought three busts from Gelder & Co., in Stepney—the one that was smashed in his shop and the two he had sold to Dr. Barnicot.

Holmes showed Hudson the photograph, and he nodded. "It's Beppo. He worked here part-time but left last week. Two days later, the bust was smashed."

Our next stop was Gelder & Co., where the smashed busts were made. It was a large factory. Workers were busy making plaster statues.

Mr. Gelder, the manager, was a tall, blond man. He told us that hundreds of the Napoleon busts had been made over the years. He checked his record book and said that three copies had been sent to Morse Hudson on June 3 of last year. They came from a batch of six. The other three had been sent to Harding Brothers.

Gelder laughed at the idea of anyone's wishing to destroy them. "They are just cheap plaster."

He showed us a table that held drying plaster forms. "We make them in two pieces and join them."

Holmes showed him the photograph. "Do you know this man?"

Gelder's face grew red. "The rascal! He worked here once. About a year ago, he knifed a man in the street. The police arrested him right here. Beppo was his first name. I never knew his last."

"What did he get?" Holmes asked.

"One year in jail. The man he stabbed lived.

Beppo's cousin works here now. He might know where Beppo is."

"No," said Holmes, "not a word to the cousin. By the way, do you remember *exactly* when Beppo was arrested?"

"I do, in fact. It was May 20—my wife's birthday." We thanked him and headed to the Harding Brothers shop. On the way, Holmes bought a newspaper. In it was an article by Horace Harker. The headline read: "Kensington Outrage. Murder by a Madman."

"Listen to what he wrote," Holmes said. "'Inspector Lestrade and Sherlock Holmes, the famous detective, believe only a madman could have committed these crimes.'"

Holmes laughed. "Newspapers are valuable, Watson, if you know how to use them."

At the Harding Brothers shop, the manager said he had read about the smashed busts. He told us he had bought three from Gelder & Co. He had sold one of the busts to Mr. Harker, as we knew. One of the other two was bought by Josiah Brown. The second was bought by a Mr. Sandeford.

We showed the manager the photograph, but he had never seen Beppo. We thanked him and hurried back to Baker Street in time to meet Lestrade.

"We have identified the dead man," Lestrade said. "He is Pietro Venucci, from Naples, Italy. He is a known cutthroat and part of a dangerous gang. We think he was after the man in the photograph, maybe because he broke gang rules. We think Venucci was trailing the man and saw him enter Harker's house. When the fellow came out, Venucci tried to knife him. In the fight, he got knifed instead. What do you think, Mr. Holmes?"

"Excellent, Lestrade!" Holmes said "But why were the busts destroyed?"

"Forget those busts! We are after a murderer. We will soon have our man."

Holmes smiled. "I think if you come with me tonight at eleven, I shall have him for you."

"Come where?"

"To Chiswick," Holmes replied.

Holmes spent the evening looking through his file of old newspapers. He never left his desk, except to go out and send a telegram.

Lestrade arrived just before eleven. Then we took a short carriage ride to a house in Chiswick. The lights were all out. The moon was bright, but a fence threw a shadow across the part of the yard where we waited in hiding.

We didn't wait long. Within 15 minutes, the yard gate swung open. A figure rushed up the path to the house. The figure paused for a moment. Then we heard a creaking sound. A window was being opened.

Soon we saw the flash of a lantern through the window. It moved from one room to another. At last, the figure that had been holding the lantern came back out. It was a man. He carried something white under his arm.

The man checked to see if anyone was coming. Then he set the white object on the ground. It was a plaster bust! He picked up a rock from the yard and threw it down on the bust. We heard the pieces rattle on the path.

The man was so busy with all of this that he never heard us. Quick as a flash, Holmes was on his back. Moments later, Lestrade had the handcuffs on him. He was the man in the photograph!

Holmes squatted on the path, examining the pieces of plaster. They all looked the same.

Then a lantern appeared in the front doorway of the house, and a man stepped out. "Mr. Josiah Brown, I believe?" said Holmes.

"Yes, sir. And you must be Mr. Sherlock Holmes. I got your telegram and did exactly as you told me. We locked every door and waited upstairs. I see you caught the rascal."

"Yes," Holmes said. "Thank you for your help."

On the way back to the police station, our prisoner wouldn't talk. But we found a long knife on him with traces of dried blood on its blade.

"He's our man," Lestrade said to Holmes. "But I

still don't know how you worked it out."

"It's late," said Holmes. "If you come by tomorrow, I'll explain. I think you will find the case is even bigger than you think."

The next evening Lestrade had more information about Beppo. He had once been a skillful sculptor and had earned an honest living. But somewhere along the line, he had turned to crime. He had gone to jail for theft. Later, as we knew, he had spent a year in jail for stabbing a man.

Beppo could speak English very well. But he refused to explain why he had smashed the busts. It seemed he might even have made those busts while he was working at Gelder & Co.

Holmes listened to Lestrade politely, but I saw his thoughts were elsewhere. Finally, Lestrade said, "Perhaps the reason he smashed the busts will always be a mystery."

Just then, there was a knock at our door. Holmes opened it, and in stepped a white-haired man. He carried a cloth bag.

Holmes said, "Mr. Sandeford, of Reading, I believe." Then he introduced us all.

Mr. Sandeford said, "You sent me a telegram about a bust that I own."

Holmes nodded.

"I have it here. You said, 'I understand you bought a plaster bust of Napoleon from Harding Brothers. I am prepared to pay 10 pounds for it.'"

"That's right," said Holmes. "Mr. Harding told me he had sold you one."

"Did he tell you how much I paid for it?" asked Sandeford.

"No, he did not," said Holmes.

"Well, I am an honest man," Sandeford said. "But I am not rich. I paid 15 shillings. You should know that before I take your 10 pounds."

"That is indeed honest of you," Holmes said. "But I have named a price, and I intend to stick to it."

"Well, here it is," Sandeford said. He opened his bag and took out the bust.

Holmes took a paper from his pocket and laid a 10-pound note on the table. "Please sign this paper, Mr. Sandeford. It says that you agree to sell all rights to the bust to me."

Sandeford signed the paper, took his 10 pounds, and said good-bye.

As soon as he left, Holmes spread a white cloth on the table and put the bust on it. Then he picked up a small hammer and smashed the bust into pieces. He leaned forward, examining the pieces closely. "Look here!" he said. He held up a piece with a round, dark object stuck to it.

"This," he said, "is the black pearl taken from the Prince of Colonna's room at the Dacre Hotel. Using my powers of deduction, I traced its strange journey. The trail ended with the last of the six busts of Napoleon made by Gelder & Co." He nodded to Lestrade. "When the Princess reported it missing, I assisted you on the case."

"I remember," said Lestrade. "We never found out where it went or who took it."

"Right," Holmes said. "The maid was a suspect, but there was no real evidence against her. Thanks to my file of old newspapers, I recalled her name: Lucretia Venucci. Her brother is Pietro Venucci, the man Beppo murdered.

"The pearl disappeared two days before Beppo was arrested for stabbing a man. He was arrested at the Gelder & Co. factory at the exact time the busts of Napoleon were being made.

"Somehow," Holmes continued, "Beppo got the pearl. He may have stolen it from Pietro. Maybe he was working with Pietro and his sister. However, it doesn't matter in this riddle.

"The main fact is that he had the pearl when the police came to the factory for him. He knew they would search him and find it. At that moment, six plaster casts of Napoleon were on the drying table. Beppo made a small hole in the wet plaster of one of them. He dropped the pearl in and, with a few touches, covered it over."

Holmes smiled grimly. "When he got out of jail a year later, the busts were scattered across London.

He didn't know which one of the busts held the pearl, but he began to track them down.

"When he went to Harker's house, Pietro Venucci followed him. My guess is that he suspected Beppo's burglary had something to do with the pearl. The two fought, and Pietro was killed."

"But if Pietro knew Beppo," I said, "why did he carry his photograph?"

"To show it to people when he was trying to track him down," Holmes said. "Anyway, with two busts remaining, I guessed Beppo would strike the one in the nearest location first. I sent a telegram to Josiah Brown to warn him. Then we set our little trap.

"When I saw the pearl wasn't in Mr. Brown's bust, I knew it had to be in Mr. Sandeford's."

We sat in silence for a moment.

Finally Lestrade spoke. "Holmes," he said, "that was brilliant. Better than our police work. But we're not jealous of you at Scotland Yard. There's not a man at the Yard that wouldn't be proud to shake your hand."

"Thank you," said Holmes, and I could see he was touched by the compliment.

"Put the pearl in the safe," he said to me. Then he turned back to Lestrade and shook his hand. "Good-bye, my friend. And if any other little problem comes your way, please call me. I shall be happy to help if I can."